W9-DJI-751

MUPPET KIDS IN
Mom's Having a Baby

By Louise Gikow

Illustrated by Tom Cooke

A GOLDEN BOOK • NEW YORK
Western Publishing Company, Inc., Racine, Wisconsin 53404

© 1991 Henson Associates, Inc. All rights reserved. Printed in the U.S.A. No part of this book may be reproduced or copied in any form without written permission from the publisher. MUPPETS and MUPPET KIDS and character names are trademarks of Henson Associates, Inc. All other trademarks are the property of Western Publishing Company, Inc. Library of Congress Catalog Card Number: 90-85938 ISBN: 0-307-12661-7/ISBN: 0-307-62661-X (lib. bdg.)   MCMXCI

"Fozzie! Breakfast time!"

"In a minute, Pop!"

A delicious smell tickled Fozzie's nose as he raced down the stairs and into the kitchen. His dad was standing in front of the stove, flipping pancakes on the griddle.

"Mmmm," said Fozzie as Pop served him a big stack. "Smells good." Fozzie looked over at Mom. Her plate was empty.

"Aren't you having any?" he asked her.

"No, not today, dear," she said with a smile. "I'm not very hungry."

That night, Fozzie's mom knocked on his bedroom door. "Fozzie?" she said. "May I come in for a minute?"

Fozzie's mom sat down on the edge of his bed. Fozzie rolled over and stared at the ceiling.

"Are you okay, Fozzie?" his mother asked. "I know the news about the baby must have been a bit of a surprise."

I'll say, Fozzie thought. But he just nodded.

Fozzie's mom gently pulled the covers up around his chin. "I love you very much, sweetheart," she said, kissing his cheek. *Then why do you need some other kid around?* Fozzie wanted to say. *You've already got me. Aren't I good enough?*

But he just turned on his side and mumbled good-night.

For a week or so, Fozzie felt hurt and confused. Everyone thought that having a new baby was a great idea — even Kermit. But what did Kermit know? *He* didn't have to share everything he owned with someone else. *His* parents weren't going to have a baby.

One evening, Fozzie had been staring at the same page in his workbook for a half hour when his mom and dad came into the living room. They were carrying his old teddy bear and some other things.

"Fozzie," Pop said, "we decided that it would be fun to practice taking care of the baby. After all, you're a big boy now, and it's been a long time since we diapered you. Come and help us."

"Well, all right," Fozzie said.

Fozzie helped his parents diaper the teddy bear. Then they gave the teddy bear a bottle and burped him and wrapped him in a blanket and put him to bed in Fozzie's old bassinet. The bassinet was in the study, only now the study was painted yellow with a blue ceiling that had little clouds on it.

That night, Fozzie's mom knocked on his bedroom door. "Fozzie?" she said. "May I come in for a minute?"

Fozzie's mom sat down on the edge of his bed. Fozzie rolled over and stared at the ceiling.

"Are you okay, Fozzie?" his mother asked. "I know the news about the baby must have been a bit of a surprise."

I'll say, Fozzie thought. But he just nodded.

Fozzie's mom gently pulled the covers up around his chin. "I love you very much, sweetheart," she said, kissing his cheek. *Then why do you need some other kid around?* Fozzie wanted to say. *You've already got me. Aren't I good enough?*

But he just turned on his side and mumbled good-night.

For a week or so, Fozzie felt hurt and confused. Everyone thought that having a new baby was a great idea — even Kermit. But what did Kermit know? *He* didn't have to share everything he owned with someone else. *His* parents weren't going to have a baby.

One evening, Fozzie had been staring at the same page in his workbook for a half hour when his mom and dad came into the living room. They were carrying his old teddy bear and some other things.

"Fozzie," Pop said, "we decided that it would be fun to practice taking care of the baby. After all, you're a big boy now, and it's been a long time since we diapered you. Come and help us."

"Well, all right," Fozzie said.

Fozzie helped his parents diaper the teddy bear. Then they gave the teddy bear a bottle and burped him and wrapped him in a blanket and put him to bed in Fozzie's old bassinet. The bassinet was in the study, only now the study was painted yellow with a blue ceiling that had little clouds on it.

"Do you think the baby will like living here?"
asked Pop.

"Sure," Fozzie said. "I guess."

"We thought you could draw the baby a pic-
ture," said Mom. "We could put it up right over
there."

"Maybe," Fozzie said.

That night, Fozzie's mom and dad came into his room to tuck him in and kiss him good-night.

"Pop," Fozzie asked in a small voice, "will you still tuck me in and kiss me good-night when the baby is here?"

"Of course we will, Fozzie," said Pop.

Fozzie swallowed. "And you'll still love me?"

Fozzie's mom put her arms around him. "Oh, Fozzie," she said. "We'll always love you. And so will the baby."

The day before the reports were due at school, Fozzie met Kermit in the lunchroom.

"What are you bringing in tomorrow?" Kermit asked. "I'm going to talk about fishing and show everyone my new fishing pole."

Fozzie sat there, thinking. He'd been so busy worrying about the new baby that he'd forgotten all about the report.

Then he had an idea.

"It's a secret," he said. "Wait and see."

The next day, Fozzie came to school with a big bag. When it was his turn to speak, he went up to the front of the room and unpacked the bag. Inside were his teddy bear, a diaper, a bottle, and a blanket.

"My family is going to have a new baby," he announced. "And my report is about all the things you have to do when a baby is living with you."

"Do you think the baby will like living here?"
asked Pop.

"Sure," Fozzie said. "I guess."

"We thought you could draw the baby a pic-
ture," said Mom. "We could put it up right over
there."

"Maybe," Fozzie said.

That night, Fozzie's mom and dad came into his room to tuck him in and kiss him good-night.

"Pop," Fozzie asked in a small voice, "will you still tuck me in and kiss me good-night when the baby is here?"

"Of course we will, Fozzie," said Pop.

Fozzie swallowed. "And you'll still love me?"

Fozzie's mom put her arms around him. "Oh, Fozzie," she said. "We'll always love you. And so will the baby."

The day before the reports were due at school, Fozzie met Kermit in the lunchroom.

"What are you bringing in tomorrow?" Kermit asked. "I'm going to talk about fishing and show everyone my new fishing pole."

Fozzie sat there, thinking. He'd been so busy worrying about the new baby that he'd forgotten all about the report.

Then he had an idea.

"It's a secret," he said. "Wait and see."

The next day, Fozzie came to school with a big bag. When it was his turn to speak, he went up to the front of the room and unpacked the bag. Inside were his teddy bear, a diaper, a bottle, and a blanket.

"My family is going to have a new baby," he announced. "And my report is about all the things you have to do when a baby is living with you."

When Fozzie and his father got to the hospital, a nurse met them outside the maternity wing.

"You'll have to wash your hands and put on this gown," she told Fozzie. "Then you can meet your new brother."

Fozzie's mom was sitting up in bed when they got to her room. She looked tired but happy, too.

"Hello, sweetheart," she said to Fozzie, giving him a big hug.

Then Pop showed Fozzie the baby. "Meet your brother, Freddie!" Pop said. "Would you like to hold him?"

"Gee, could I?" Fozzie said.

"Of course. After all, he's *your* brother," said Pop. "Just sit down there. Now, careful of his head."

"*I* know," Fozzie said. He gently cradled the baby in his arms.

Three days later, Mom and Freddie came home. Fozzie helped put the baby into the bassinet.

"Hey, Freddie," Fozzie said, after the baby was tucked in. "Why did the chicken cross the road?"

The baby's face crinkled. "He smiled!" gasped Fozzie. "I'm sure he smiled."

Then Fozzie looked up at Mom and Pop. "You know what?" he said. "This baby and I are going to get along just fine."